ANNO'S
FLEA MARKET

Mitsumasa Anno

PHILOMEL BOOKS
NEW YORK

Other Books by Mitsumasa Anno
published by Philomel Books

Anno's Animals
Anno's Britain
Anno's Counting House
Anno's Italy
Anno's Journey
Anno's Magical ABC:
An Anamorphic Alphabet
Anno's Medieval World
Anno's Mysterious Multiplying Jar
Anno's U.S.A.
The King's Flower
The Unique World of Mitsumasa Anno:
Selected Works (1968-1977)

First USA edition 1984. Published by Philomel Books, a division of The Putnam Publishing Group, 51 Madison Avenue, New York NY 10010. Text translation copyright © 1984 by Philomel Books. Original Japanese edition published in 1983 by Dowaya, Tokyo, copyright © 1983 by Kuso-Kubo. All rights reserved. Translation rights were arranged with Dowaya through the Kurita-Bando Literary Agency. Printed in Japan. Library of Congress Cataloging in Publication Data at back of book.

Prologue

Every Saturday morning in this town the great central square is filled with street stalls, booths and tables, and with men, women and children buying or selling almost everything you can imagine. There are farmers selling fresh fruits and vegetables. Other people are selling things for everyday use like pots and pans, or chairs and tables. There are new things and old, treasures and trash, even such things as worn-out light bulbs, old eyeglass frames without lenses, run-down clocks, trumpets with broken mouthpieces, and rusty, old-fashioned tools. Yet each of these old things has a tale to tell us if we will stop to listen. Each has been used in the past by someone's grandmother or great-grandfather or mother.

Among these old things you will find some you'd like to pick up, to handle, to bargain for, perhaps to own. Another object will make you shake your head and give up trying to guess what it could be. Who would buy such a useless thing? But never fear — someone else will come along who knows just the use for this rejected object. So look carefully at the things in this flea market. They will tell you fascinating tales of long ago and far away, of the people who made them and those who used them.

You can pick your own pathway to the past as you explore the crowded stalls of this flea market. Did you notice the old man and woman with their laden handcart? When I saw them at the beginning and again at the ending of a French film directed by René Clair, I thought they, too, must be heading for my flea market. Join them on an imaginary journey through space and time — a journey through the fourth dimension into the enchanted world of the past.

spinach
l'épinard

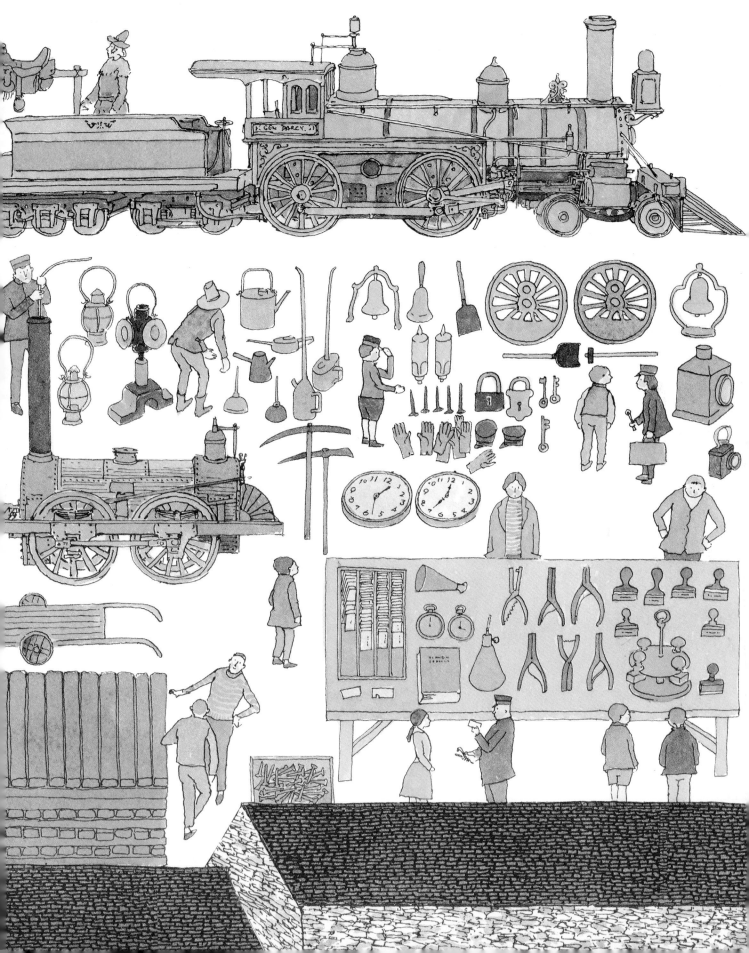

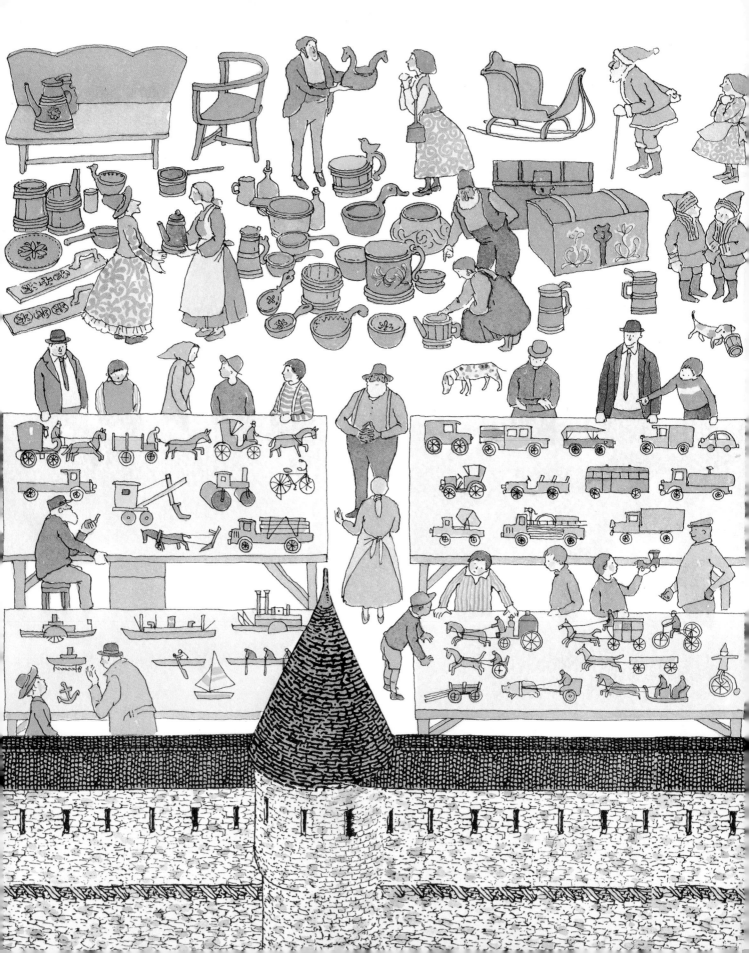

Epilogue

I would like to be able to show you a wooden bowl I have—a wide, deep bowl that was once used for kneading dough. It was made by scooping out a solid piece of a large tree trunk to its present, particularly appealing form. It would be hard to find such a kneading bowl now, unless, like me, you happen to enjoy visiting flea markets.

One day, in a market very much like the one in this book, my eye was caught by this old bowl, its patina glowing softly through the dust that covered it, and I began to wonder about the girl who had used it long ago. This led to thoughts of the woodcarver who had got the wood out of the forest—and this, in turn, led to thoughts about the tree itself. After so much wondering and speculation about the bowl, naturally I couldn't resist buying it!

Somehow we are born with a sixth sense that enables us to distinguish things that are handmade and original from their mass-produced imitations. We have some inner circuitry that detects the new, the reproduction, the false, and separates it from the old and genuine. Some people go to great effort to make a brand-new thing look old and worn; indeed, it must be very difficult to produce these spurious copies of handmade artifacts in large quantities! But somehow the inner beauty of the old and authentic object makes itself felt to those who are sensitive to it, just as my beloved wooden bowl evokes in me thoughts of its first owner and user, and of the craftsperson who carved its satisfying proportions.

This book was first published in 1984. You could call it a new book, yes, but only for a little while. If it is your own book, write in it the date when you received it, and make notes of the things you observed when you first looked through it. I'll be happy if you return to my flea market in this book after a long period of time. I wonder if it will look the same to you then, or if you will find new treasures there? Perhaps, one day, in a real flea market you may even find a copy of this very book on sale, who knows?

—Mitsumasa Anno